Hold Me For Now

A Dark Romance Novella

Lexi Davis

The story, all names, characters, and incidents portrayed in this production are fictitious. No identification with actual persons (living or deceased), places, buildings, and products is intended or should be inferred.

Book Covers by The Author Buddy

Copyediting by Dymond and Associates

Copyright © 2025 by Lexi Davis

All rights reserved. No part of this publication may be reproduced, distributed, or transmitted in any form or by any means, including photocopying, recording, or other electronic or mechanical methods, without the prior written permission of the author, except for the use of brief quotations in articles or book reviews and as permitted by U.S. copyright law.

ISBN (eBook) 979-8-9925298-4-5

ISBN (Paperback photo cover) 979-8-9925298-5-2

ISBN (Paperback discrete/flower cover) 979-8-9925298-6-9

Contents

Foreword	V
Dedication	VII
1. Chapter 1	1
2. Chapter 2	6
3. Chapter 3	11
4. Chapter 4	17
5. Chapter 5	23
6. Chapter 6	26
7. Chapter 7	31
8. Chapter 8	40
9. Chapter 9	43
10. Chapter 10	48
11. Chapter 11	54
12. Chapter 12	57

13. Epilogue   62

14. Acknowledgments   75

Foreword

Trigger Warnings / Author Note *(Contains Mild Spoilers)*

Your mental health matters to me. Please check the trigger warnings before reading.

This is a work of *FICTION*. If you have medical trauma or discomfort around clinical settings, this book may not be the right fit—and that's okay. My goal is never to make you feel unsafe. One of the things I love most about writing romance is giving readers a safe space to explore taboo topics and to push emotional boundaries. If this story isn't for you, I understand completely and support whatever reading decisions you make.

With love,

XOXO, Lexi

Trigger Warnings

This book contains:

- Vulnerable explorations of intimacy and identity

- Discussions about sexual dysfunction and performance pressure

- Clinical sex therapy as a central setting

- A married character navigating separation/divorce

- References to past toxic relationships

- Themes of low self-worth, shame, and learning to speak up for your needs

- Emotionally intense, open-door sexual content

- Explicit language

- Emotional manipulation (not by the main characters)

- Voyeurism (for clinical purposes only—non-arousing and professional)

While all intimacy in this story is consensual and healing-focused, it explores emotionally complex situations and unconventional dynamics in a clinical setting. Please take care while reading. This book was written with empathy, hope—and a whole lot of heart.

Dedication

Dedication:

For the ones who never learned how to ask for what they wanted.
For the people pleasers, the overthinkers, the ones who stay quiet even when they're screaming inside.
I see you.
Please know you deserve someone who knows all of you—and stays.

***

"I've been the archer, I've been the prey. Who could ever leave me, darling? But who could stay?"
–The Archer, Taylor Alison Swift

***

CONNECT ON SOCIAL MEDIA—LET'S BE FRIENDS

Instagram, TikTok, Facebook: @authorlexidavis

Chapter One

My heart pounds with nervous anticipation, a dull, heavy drumbeat. I take in a shuddering breath and survey the room. It's sterile, white, devoid of anything except one single piece of furniture.

A bed.

Set in the very center of the room. It's not on a raised dais or under a spotlight, but still I have the impression that it's a stage. A place where actors perform. Except, I guess in this twisted little drama *I'm* the star of the show.

My stomach clenches at the thought, and my fingers curl into fists at my sides. Every instinct screams at me to leave, to rip open the door and run until the cool outside air chokes my lungs.

A voice crackles from the speaker, cutting through the silence.

"It'll be just a few more minutes, Kristi. The other patient is almost here."

I jump, pulse hammering, startled by the disembodied voice. It comes from a speaker high on the wall, right above the only other feature. A one-way mirror. Opaque to me, but transparent to him. That's how he'll watch us.

Dr. Desire.

That's what he calls himself. I'll never know his real name. He'd been clear about that in our email communications. Not only will I never see his face, but I'm pretty sure he's using a voice changer, so I won't even know what he sounds like.

That's okay, as long as he fixes me.

With a sinking heart, I realize that's how desperate I've become.

My problem is so unusual, so embarrassing. When I posted about it anonymously, I'd never expected anyone to answer me. I still don't know how Dr. Desire had plucked me out of the sex chat forum or how he'd discovered my real name and email address. His response had reeled me in with one simple, damning promise.

His subject line had read, "I can get you to orgasm, 100% guaranteed."

Of course, at first I'd laughed, thinking it was just another pervert, trying to come on to me over the Internet.

"Yeah, right," I'd responded sarcastically. "Let me guess, with your huge cock."

To which he'd written back, "No, I'm not going to have sex with you. I have another patient with the same problem. If you meet the criteria, I'll guide both of you through intercourse until you're cured. I've used this technique many times with great success."

He'd attached a detailed questionnaire as well as testimonials from what he claimed were hundreds of satisfied clients.

I'd downloaded the survey on a whim and filled it out. The questions were thorough.

Disturbingly so.

There were the usual ones. *How many sexual partners have you had? When did you first experience an orgasm?*

Then more specific ones. *Do you have a preference in the size/shape of your partner's penis? Which breast is more sensitive?*

I'd paused at that, thinking how ridiculous it was. Then I squeezed my left breast, followed by my right. Turns out that my left, the slightly bigger one, is more easily stimulated.

Who knew?

When I emailed the answers back, I pretended like I didn't care, didn't even think this was anything more than some deranged weirdo getting his jollies from reading about my sex life. But time passed, and I found myself obsessively checking my email, wondering if Dr. Desire would accept me into his "specialty clinic."

On the seventh day, I'd received his answer.

An address that led to this nondescript building in an industrial part of the city.

A code that opened the door to this strange room.

Now, I wait. Dreading. Hoping.

A glance at my watch. I've been here five minutes already. I tell myself to be patient, not a particular virtue of mine, and resume nervously wringing my hands. My gaze darts to the one-way mirror, wondering who could be on the other side.

There's a beeping from behind me. I whirl just as the door swings open. A man walks in, his shoulders hunched and his cheeks flushed red. He's decent-looking, taller than average, with wavy brown hair and warm brown eyes.

It's his clothing that takes him from "hottie" to "meh" real fast. His jeans are too whitewashed. His button-down shirt is too stiff, the collar too sharply ironed. Scuffed brown loafers give him a wholesome vibe.

I cast a critical eye over him, wondering who picked out that outfit. The whole look screams Mom-approved, like he's a teenager forced into something "nice" for Sunday school.

Definitely *not* what you'd wear to fuck a stranger.

Of course, I shouldn't judge. My fashion sense tends toward punk with a touch of goth. Today, my hair is dyed black as midnight, my skirt barely skims mid-thigh, and my fishnet stockings have a hole in one knee. I like to tell my friends I tore the stocking on purpose because I can't stand anything too perfect, but that's a lie. The truth is I tripped on my way to class at NYU and skinned my knee, like some four-year-old on the playground. One nice thing about living in New York is that people mind their own business. No one asked what happened or if they could help when I hobbled along with blood gushing down my leg. Of course...that's also the bad thing about living in New York.

This guy who just walked in—he doesn't live here. Dr. Desire said he deliberately paired us because we were "geographically separate" and wouldn't ever have to see each other after today. The doctor also said he picked us because we were "emotionally and physically compatible." I'd spent a lot of time wondering what that means but still hadn't come up with a good answer.

Guess I'm about to find out.

Chapter Two

The man has spotted me, not a hard feat since I'm the only living thing in the room. His steps falter before he forces himself forward. He approaches with his hand out to shake mine. "Hi. I'm—"

"No real names," Dr. Desire interrupts, his voice sharp as a scalpel.

The man stops like he just ran into a brick wall. The hand that was reaching for me falls, and his cheeks stain an even brighter shade of red. His Adam's apple bobs as he swallows hard. "Oh…er…I feel like we need to call each other something…?" He trails off uncertainly.

"Let's use initials," I suggest, taking one step toward him. Sympathy stirs in me. He's just as lost in this situation as I am. "My name—initial—is K." It takes my full concentration to leave it at that. The habit of saying my full name is so strong.

"I'm T," he says stiffly, snapping his mouth shut after that single letter, as if he can trap the rest of his name in his mouth.

"Nice to meet you," I say pleasantly and shake his hand.

"You too."

Now that we're closer, I look him over some more. Tan skin like he works outdoors. Large hands. Clean cut, but there's a tiny scab at the base of his throat like he nicked himself shaving. Hair cropped short, allowing slightly pointed ears to peek out.

I breathe out a sigh, relieved. I can work with those ears. I read *a lot* of smutty fantasy—fairy porn, as my friend Veronica calls it. The heroes in those books are always ridiculously hot fae warriors who steal human women away to their glittering courts.

Maybe if I imagine T as a fairy prince, one cursed, perhaps, then I can get through the next few hours and walk out of here a new woman.

"You may begin," says Dr. D—I've decided to call him that. If the rest of us are going by our first initial, he might as well too.

"Umm," hedges T, giving me enough time to wonder if it's *Ted, Tim, Tom*?

T directs his question to the mirror. "What exactly are we supposed to do? A little instruction would be helpful, please."

There's a hint of impatience when Dr. D answers, "As I stated in the email, you two will engage in sexual intercourse. I will watch and provide direction when needed."

T's brown eyes find my green ones as his brow puckers in confusion.

"How exactly are we supposed to have—" he stumbles over the word, his eyes shifting from mine, "—intercourse?"

"However you like. The details will be left to you and Ms. K to work out. Each couple is different. I find that you two coming together organically works better than me laying out each step for you. My role is purely supportive. When I see areas that could use assistance, I'll chime in." That's the most we've heard Dr. D speak so far.

T rubs the back of his neck with one hand, staring at the floor as if it might provide answers.

A thought occurs to me, one that could explain his awkwardness. "Have you…have you never done it before?"

That makes his head snap up. "Yes," he says, his voice too loud, too indignant. "Lots of times."

I hold up my hands. "Sorry! I didn't mean to assume. I just thought, well, I wondered…"

I've pissed T off. He crosses his arms over his chest defensively and declares, "I'm married, so I have sex all the time."

Those words slam into me, a physical force. I stumble backward, shocked.

Married?

"My wife—or I'm not sure what to call her. We—we're separated. Lawyers are involved. She's the reason I'm here. She said she's sick of my excuses about this problem. She said the only chance I have to get her back is to do this."

Dr. D's voice interrupts us. "I can confirm that T's spouse is on board with today's treatment. I've had extensive discussions with her myself, to make sure she understands what will happen here. She's given her verbal and written consent to proceed. I don't want to put more pressure on you than there already is, but she's rather eager to move forward. I believe she seeks a resolution to her and T's marital status."

Jesus. No pressure indeed.

"You see why I have to fix myself? Like right *now*? I need to make her happy." T's voice rises, high and tight with frustration, drawing my attention back to him. "But it's not easy. I've been everywhere. Tried everything. The result is always the same."

"So you can't," I lower my voice, which is silly. We both know why we're here. "You can't orgasm either?"

T stiffens, his nostrils flaring slightly. "I can—just only by myself. Not with her."

He runs a hand over his face, then down the back of his neck. Frustration, shame, something deeper war behind those brown eyes.

"How about other people?" I ask, confused by how he phrased his answer.

A small shake of his head. "Dunno. My wife and I are high-school sweethearts. I've never been with anyone else."

That hits like a hammer. I squeak out, "Never?"

"*Never*," he says emphatically.

Again, I have the urge to flee. It's too much pressure. To be the second lover this man, this stranger, has ever had.

He's watching me, gauging my reaction, like he's waiting for me to call him a freak. To laugh at him. To make him feel even less than he already does. I calm my expression and hide the turmoil in my mind.

"How about you?" T asks.

It's a fair question, but something about it makes my throat tighten. I duck my head, my fingers twisting in the hem of my skirt. "Same. I can get myself off but haven't had any luck doing it with other people."

Silence stretches between us, so heavy it's almost unbearable. I force myself to look up.

"Have you tried a lot?" His voice is careful, but the words hit like a slap.

My spine stiffens. "Are you asking me how many people I've slept with?" Defensively, I spit out, "Because the answer is that it's none of your business."

His brows pull together, his lips parting like he hadn't expected that reaction. "I—no, I wasn't—" He exhales sharply, rubbing a hand over his jaw. "You're right. That was out of line. I wasn't trying to judge you."

His voice dips lower, something raw edging into it. "I just meant... I've wondered if maybe I had more experience, I wouldn't have this problem."

For a second, I don't know how to respond. The despair in his voice, the barely concealed self-loathing, twists in my stomach.

I get it. I *really* get it.

But I'm still pissed.

I cross my arms, my voice tight. "Well, maybe. Or maybe experience doesn't mean shit when your body refuses to cooperate."

His eyes darken, his jaw flexing like he wants to argue but doesn't know how.

Good. Let him sit in that discomfort.

Because that's what this is, isn't it? Two broken people, thrown into a room together, expected to somehow *fix* each other.

Like it's that simple.

Chapter Three

An awkward silence descends. My gaze is drawn like a magnet to the bed. T's looking at it too.

It sits there. The elephant in the room.

"I told my wife—ex—that I couldn't do this," T blurts out of nowhere. "She insisted I come. I said absolutely not—that I wouldn't do it. I fought with her a lot, but she went ahead and found Dr. Desire anyway. She arranged everything. It's been driving her nuts, thinking something's wrong with her, even though I've told her a million times there's not."

He hangs his head. There's defeat etched in his posture, in the forward slump of his body. "I told her it's all me. *My* fault that things are falling apart."

The rawness in his voice tightens something deep in my chest. I recognize that kind of pain like it's my own. I know how blame wraps around your throat, choking you. How guilt sticks like cement on your ribs, binding them together so you can't breathe.

Without thinking, I step closer and rest my hand on his arm. T stiffens beneath my touch, his muscles taut as if he's bracing for rejection.

I hold steady, my voice quiet but certain. "It's okay," I tell him. "That's why we're here. To figure this out. Everything is going to be fine."

He relaxes at that. Slowly, his shoulders ease downward. His breath hitches, but not in that panicked way from before. This time, it's something softer.

"Thanks," he murmurs. Hesitantly, he covers my hand with his own.

That's when I feel it.

That *zing* of attraction.

My breath catches. *Oh*.

I send a silent *thank you* to the ceiling. This was one of my greatest fears, that I'd come here to find some old guy with three-foot-long nose hair that I'd have to screw. It shows how messed up I am, that even with that terrifying image in my mind, I still showed up.

I think T feels it too, that connection, because his eyes fix on me and dilate. He's been so anxious up to now that I don't think he actually saw me, but suddenly his gaze dances over my face, lingering on my hair, and then down my body, over my short skirt with its metal studs and finally to my scuffed biker boots.

I smirk, relieved to focus on something besides the fact that I'm about to fuck this dude. "Guess I'm not what you were expecting?"

His eyes fly up to mine, and he reddens at being caught staring. "I—I wasn't sure what to expect, but I'm glad it's you." He drops his gaze and mumbles, "You're pretty. I like your hair."

I laugh, the sound loud and echoing in this small room. "You don't have to flatter me," I tease. "You're already going to get me in bed."

That was the wrong thing to say. T's mouth thins into a tight line. "That wasn't flattery. I meant it."

And now things are awkward again.

Shit.

I scramble to fix it, to make amends. "Sorry. I'm just nervous. Humor is my go-to defense mechanism."

"It's okay." He's looking at me again, which I suppose means I'm forgiven. "How should we start?" A furtive glance at the bed.

I toy with the thick silver chain that serves as a belt for my skirt. "I'm not sure." My nerves ramp up, making my heart thud painfully. "Undress? Kiss? Are we allowed to kiss? Are there rules? Is there anything you want to do? Don't want to do? Should we talk about it? Plan it out? Or just go for it?" I'm babbling now. I know it, but I can't seem to stop.

T shoots a look at the mirror. "Dr. Desire? Any input?"

The voice comes out of the speaker, deep and slightly distorted. "It's up to you. There are no right or wrong answers. That's an important lesson when it comes to sex."

I release a deep breath and shake out my shoulders. "Let's start by kissing," I suggest. "Maybe that'll get us in the mood."

He faces me, his throat bobbing. "Okay. Let's do it."

We shuffle toward each other until we're face to face. Too close. Not close enough. Hesitantly, T reaches out and frames my face with his hands. He has calloused fingers that ghost along my cheekbone. The contrast of rough against smooth sends a ripple down my spine.

Eyes searching, he asks a silent question, a request.

I nod.

He lowers his mouth to mine. Warm breath and soft lips, a gentle kiss. T smells strongly of mint, as if he ate an entire pack of Altoids on his way over here.

A sigh escapes me at the sweetness of it. I can't remember the last time, if ever, that someone kissed me like this. That someone touched me so delicately, as if they were afraid to break me.

But I'm not fragile, and, as nice as this is, it's not going to get us into bed. Which is what I desperately need because if this doesn't work...I don't know what I'll do.

I part my lips and let my tongue flick over his bottom lip, tasting the heat of him. T inhales sharply, his breath shuddering against my mouth like he wasn't expecting this. That split-second hesitation is all the invitation I need. I slide my tongue past his lips, catching another startled gasp—hot and sharp, it spills into me. I drink it down greedily, like I can steal a part of him, take his breath, his need, his hesitation, and make it mine.

The kiss shifts. It starts out chaste and then ignites into a three-alarm fire.

T's fingers slip into my hair. Without hesitation, he palms the back of my head and deepens the kiss, leaning his long, thin frame against my shorter one. Now I'm the one surprised by the pressure of his body, by the intensity of his mouth moving against mine. I had pegged him for a bit of a country bumpkin. I had assumed that only being with one woman would make him inexperienced, but I was so wrong.

This man.

He knows how to kiss a woman.

Arousal shoots up my spine, quickens my breath, and makes me moan, a quiet whimper.

That single sound, so unplanned, breaks the spell between us.

T stumbles away from me with wide, shocked eyes. His hand flies up to his mouth, fingers pressing against his lips like he can still feel me there.

On instinct, I go to chase him but stop myself, which is unusual for me. I'm always the one who pursues. The one to make the first move. To be the aggressor. It's occurred to me recently that maybe that's part of my problem. Why I always end up with the assholes, the users. Perhaps I force acts, relationships, that were never meant to be?

This time will be different, I decide. After all, T's nothing like the guys I've dated in the past.

Not that I'm dating him, of course.

This is just sex.
Nothing more.

Chapter Four

I put my hands up, showing him my empty palms like I'm trying to convince him I hold no weapons.

"I'm—I'm sorry," he stutters. "I just—I wasn't expecting that...and wow. You're a good kisser, but it feels so strange. Like I'm cheating, but I'm not. I—I don't know how to handle this."

"I get it," I reassure him, attempting to put myself in his shoes. "As weird as this is for me, I'm single. Haven't had a steady boyfriend in over two years. It must be *way* more difficult for you."

He quirks his head at that, eyes sharpening. "Two years?"

I let out a nervous, high-pitched laugh. Exposed and vulnerable, I wonder why of all the things I just said, *that's* the detail he latches on to. "Yeah...it's been a while."

"But how can you be sure you can't—you know—orgasm if it's been that long?"

I laugh again. This time sharper, with a bitter edge. Sarcastically, I say, "Oh, you sweet, naïve man. Just because I haven't had a boyfriend doesn't mean I haven't had sex." I hold his gaze, daring him to react. "I've had *lots*. Made it my mission, really, trying to figure out what's wrong with me."

That makes T frown, his mouth bracketed by deep curved lines in the corners.

I break off my chuckling abruptly, sure that he's judging me. Crossing my arms over my chest, I send him a glare. "No slut shaming, please. That's *so* early 2000s."

A guilty flush climbs his neck. "Sorry. I wasn't—well, maybe I *was* thinking that, and you're right. I shouldn't judge. I know how bad that feels. Lots of people give me grief, say I'm stupid for only ever being with one woman."

Now *I* feel awful, because I *did* think that about him, that he must have low standards to settle for the first girl to wet his dick.

"I'm sorry too," I admit. "It's easy to throw stones at other people's choices and ignore the glass walls that surround us, isn't it?"

T's head bobs in a nod. His gaze grows distant, wistful. "I know what people think of me, that I'm pathetic, that I must not have had options, but that's not it. I chose this. I have this belief that there's someone special out there for everyone. True love—two people designed just for each other. I imagine when they find each other, everything flows. It fits, clicks, like a key sliding into a lock."

Warmth unfurls in my chest at the idea that there's a perfect someone out there waiting for me. It's a total fantasy, of course, but, God, do I wish it were true. "I like that," I tell T, meaning it. I offer him a small, genuine smile. "I hope you can get the key to your lock back, that things work out between you."

Something dark flits across his expression, gone before I can name it. He gives me the ghost of a smile and says, "Thanks."

"Focus, please. We're getting off track," says the disembodied voice of Dr. D.

T and I both jump at the sound. I'd almost forgotten we weren't alone. A flash of irritation tenses my muscles. Doesn't he understand we need this? A chance to connect emotionally before we connect physically. At least *I* need it.

"Sorry," T says to the speaker high on the wall. He moves toward me, more determined now. "Let's try again. Promise I won't freak out this time."

Now that I know what a good kisser he is, my pulse skips with anticipation as I rise up on my toes and wind my arms around his neck. I'm about to say something witty or comforting or I don't know what because T doesn't give me a chance. His lips crash into me. No hesitation this time. No careful testing of the waters. His tongue sweeps against mine, demanding, devouring, kissing the hell out of me.

A whimper escapes me, raw and feral.

And *fuck*, that does something to him.

His fingers twist in my hair, tightening. His lean, solid frame presses into me, and now I feel his heat, his urgency, the way his body reacts like it's spiraling out of control.

This isn't just a kiss.

It's not him doing it to prove he can or because it's what's expected.

This is *need*.

Pure, raw, *hunger*.

We break apart, breathless. I lick my lips, dazed. Because I can't help myself, I tease, "Dang! You were holding back on me the first time, T."

"Fuck, yeah, I was." His voice is rough and low, gravel sliding over silk. Then he's back, ravaging me with his tongue, and, holy shit, it's *hot*.

"Touch her breast, the left one," says Dr. D.

So engrossed in what we're doing, we barely flinch at the intrusion. T follows the instructions immediately. His hand comes up to cup and knead my breast over my shirt. He locates my peaked nipple through the thin fabric of my sheer blouse and black bra and runs his fingers over it. I moan into his mouth. An ache pulses between my legs.

My hands find the hem of his shirt and slip beneath it. His abs are hard, well-defined. I wonder if he works out or just works outside. Something that involves manual labor. Construction maybe? I want to ask, to know more about him, but remind myself that's not why we're here. This isn't about making a love connection. It's about making me come during sex.

Focus, I tell myself. *Eyes on the prize.*

T mimics me, sliding his hand under my shirt. Rough fingers trace my ribs as he glides his palm along my skin. He reaches around my back and, after a minute of fumbling, unclasps my bra. It gapes loose on my chest, which allows him to touch my breast by shoving his hand under the cup. Heeding Dr. Desire's advice, he goes for my left breast first. His hand is so big, he easily covers my entire breast, encasing it with his warmth. He's not gentle, which I like. T pinches my nipple, rubs it with the pad of his thumb, and somehow it feels like he's also touching me down there, between my legs.

I break off our kiss to lick down his neck while my hands explore under his shirt, tracing the contours of his muscles, which shift as his breath catches, then speeds. Wanting better access, I shove his shirt up. With a petulant scowl, I demand, "Off! Take it off!"

He chuckles, and, for the first time, I see him truly smile. It's like a burst of sunlight breaking through storm clouds—warm, effortless, charming. His whole face transforms, eyes crinkling at the corners, tension melting away. I go still, caught off guard by the sight. This feels like the real T. The version of him not weighed down by anxiety, guilt, or doubt. I can see how he belongs in this light, at ease in a world I can never seem to reach.

I'm not like that. I carry the weight of reality like a second skin, unable to ignore the world's sharp edges, its subtle cruelties. Darkness clings to me, a familiar presence I've learned to live with. Maybe that's why I want this so badly—to connect with someone else, to be truly intimate. If I can break this barrier and experience pleasure the way I'm supposed to, maybe it will finally chase my shadows away.

T bends down, bringing his face to mine. "Ladies first," he says with a twinkle in his eyes. He reaches for the bottom of my shirt and catches it between his fingers. I raise my hands over my head so he can pull it off, which he does in one smooth motion. My bra comes with it so now I'm naked from the waist up. The air in the room has a sharp chill to it, which raises goosebumps along my arms. The cold is a reality check, making me acutely aware that I'm the only half-naked person in the room. A sudden wave of self-consciousness washes over me, and I instinctively cross my arms over my chest, shielding myself.

T lifts a brow, his gaze catching the movement.

"I'm just cold," I say, the excuse feeble.

"Sure," he replies easily, but the way his eyes narrow, how he holds me in his stare, makes me feel more exposed than ever. There's something unspoken between us. Me, silently pleading for understanding, and him seeing straight through me.

Without a word, he reaches for the hem of his shirt and pulls it over his head. "There," he says, his voice steady. He goes straight to the heart of my unease. "Now we're even."

Relief floods through me. He understood. He didn't call me out on my vulnerability. Instead, he met it with his own. I want to say thanks, but I'm too busy scanning his perfect six-pack, his muscular shoulders, the scattering of gold-dusted hair over his chest and stomach that leads down like an arrow pointing to his crotch. My gaze snags on that area, noting the sizable bulge that strains the zipper of his jeans.

Jesus.

T sees where I'm looking and blushes bright red. He angles his body away, hiding whatever resides in those jeans. He coughs into his hand and clears his throat.

And we're back to being awkward again. Me with my arms covering my breasts. Him hiding his erection. For a minute, I wonder if we're really going to be able to do this. We might both be too insecure, too overwhelmed, to make it happen.

Chapter Five

Dr. D must be thinking the same thing. His voice is overly loud in the small space. "You two are doing great," he encourages. "Let's not lose this momentum. Help each other take off your clothes."

Neither of us reacts to his request. Instead, we eye each other warily. Tension rises, broken when T flicks his eyes to the speaker in the wall. "Can we—uh—can we like dim the lights or something? It's kinda bright in here."

He's right, of course. It's like a thousand suns shine down on us, with all the fluorescent lights recessed into the ceiling. It gives the room a clinical, hospital feel. Not exactly something that sparks romance.

Dr. D sounds apologetic when he responds with a hurried, "Oh! Of course. Here you go." The lights dim, settle down to a glow. Shadows soften enough that I let my arms drop. I reach down for the zipper on my skirt, but strong fingers beat me there.

"Here." T's voice is husky and low. "Let me help." There's something sensual about how slowly he unzips me, about how he helps to shimmy my skirt over my hips and down to my ankles. I step out of it and stand only in my boots and fishnet stockings. No underwear.

T licks his lips. Unblinking, he stares at me with his chest rising and falling rapidly. "I think I dreamed about this once," he murmurs. His voice is distant, like he's slipped into a trance.

There's no change in his expression or the way his eyes explore my body when I unbutton his pants and unzip him. Before I can pull them down, he knocks my hand away. Staring at the ground, his jaw tense, T mumbles, "I don't want you to be turned off. I'm kinda big. My wife says it's too much, that it's…unnatural."

A semihysterical laugh climbs my throat along with 500 sarcastic comments, but I swallow them down. He's serious about this, insecure about his body. A tiny flare of anger lights in my chest at this unknown woman—his wife—who planted this doubt in his mind.

I hook my fingers into the belt loops of his jeans and tug him toward the bed. "Why don't you let me be the judge of that?"

Walking backward, I tow him along until the back of my legs hits the edge of the bed. I sit, my face at the level of his stomach. Tilting my head up to stare into T's eyes, I pull his pants down to his knees. His erection springs free. I can see it in my peripheral vision, but I don't look at it. Without taking my eyes off him, I lean down and take him into my mouth. T's eyes go round with shock, then slide closed as his chest heaves. He groans, deep and guttural. That sound travels straight to my core, where wetness pools.

I have a few things I pride myself on. Singing the alphabet backward, getting a perfect score on the verbal section of the SAT, and giving mind-bending blow jobs. Even my shittiest of boyfriends have commented on how I give the best head. Full of my own confidence, I take T deep, choking a bit because, although he's not the biggest I've ever had, he's definitely in the top three. I curl my lips over my teeth so I don't hurt him and bob up and down on his cock, letting it slide down the back of my throat with every dip of my head.

"Holy fuck." T winds his fingers into my hair, clasping my head as I work. I brace myself, waiting for him to force me deeper, to shove my face against his nuts like so many men have done in the past, but he doesn't. He just cups my head and brushes his thumbs over my temples in slow circles. I close my fist around his shaft and squeeze gently while my other hand comes up to cup his balls. T groans again, his body tensing like he's close to coming. I ready myself to swallow but don't get the chance because that's when Dr. D interrupts.

"Let's move on from oral sex," he says, almost like he's bored. "I want this session to focus on penetration as the vehicle that leads to orgasm. You've both reported that as your greatest challenge. Please finish undressing and then I'd like you to get in bed together."

Chapter Six

T pulls back, his chest heaving and his expression dazed. "Damn, K. That was amazing."

Pride warms my insides. I toss my hair and smirk. "I know. It's kind of my specialty."

I expect him to laugh, like he did earlier, but instead something angry, almost possessive, flickers in the depth of his eyes. Jaw working, he turns away, giving me a view of his very fine ass. With his back to me, he steps out of his jeans and underwear, then neatly folds them and bends down to put them on the floor.

When T finally faces me again, there's a distance between us, a wariness in his expression. I'm not sure what I did to deserve it. It shouldn't bother me, his sudden frostiness. I don't even know this guy. I'll never see him again. It hurts my feelings somehow, like he's rejecting me before I've even had him. My spirits plummet, and sadness creeps in.

Refusing to look at him, I lean over to untie my boots. I've got the knot undone on the first one when T drops to his knees before me. Deft fingers untie my other boot with lightning speed. He holds the back of my calf and yanks off one boot, followed by the next. He rises to his full height, reminding me just how tall he is.

"Lean back," T says, his voice gruff.

I do as he says, laying on my back with my legs dangling over the edge. He grips the top of my stockings and pulls. I lift my hips, deliberately staring at the ceiling, as he drags my tights off until I'm completely naked. The bed dips as he climbs in next to me. T helps me shift up higher until my head lands on the thin pillow. The mattress creaks, the sound loud in the silence. A whisper of fabric signals the sheet being drawn up. He pulls it over my body in a clumsy attempt at modesty, covering me from the shoulders down. I roll onto my side, facing him as he settles onto the other pillow, burrowing under the sheet.

My hair has spilled across my cheek, tangling from all the movement. T brushes it aside with a soft, "Hey." His expression is sympathetic, like he understands the snarled knots of my emotions because he feels the same way.

"This is so weird, right?"

I gust out a startled laugh, the sound bursting free, easing the tension in my chest. "Yeah. I'm never telling anyone I did this. Like *never ever.*"

He chuckles with me, the sound of our laughter blending into one, filling the empty space between us. "Same here. *Never.*"

I roll onto my back, but the weight of his eyes stays on me, heavy and warm. Unwavering.

"Do you—do you want to stop?" he asks in a way that lets me know he hopes the answer is no.

I heave a sigh. My voice is raw, stripped down to the truth. "I don't think I can. I need this to work. Not being able to do it makes me feel broken, and I *hate* that."

T moves to hover over me, braced on one elbow. "Same," he whispers, a repeat from earlier, but this time with more emotion. A single tentative finger reaches out to stroke down my arm, leaving behind a fiery trail.

"Kiss her. Take control for now, T." Dr. D's voice rings out, and there's a sense of relief. I agree with him. It's time to take this to the next level.

"Is that okay?" T asks quietly, barely moving his mouth as if he wants to keep the question between the two of us, not to be shared with Dr. D.

I reach for him, letting my lips part. He kisses me, soft at first but building slowly until we're a mix of tongues and sighs. A strange longing for him, this man I just met, sweeps through me. T drags his hand down my body, stopping briefly to tease my nipple and then trailing it across my navel. Finally, he's between my legs.

His breath stutters when he feels how wet I am down there, but his hand doesn't hesitate. He strokes into me, running the flat of his hand from front to back, and then to the front again where, after a moment of fumbling, he finds my clit. My back arches off the bed as he teases that sensitive bundle of nerves. I'm panting now, my fingers digging into his shoulder. Inhuman whimpers burst out as he moves faster.

"You like that, don't you?" he murmurs in my ear, his breath tickling and warm. "Right there?"

"Yes." I bite my lip, letting my hips move to his rhythm. "Yes, that's it."

His erection is pressed against my side. I turn to him and grasp it tightly, noting how it grows even more rigid at my touch. We kiss, breathless, our hands busy between us.

"If you're both okay with it, T, why don't you move on top of K?" Dr. D suggests. An annoyed growl rises from the back of T's throat. He was into this, and I don't think he appreciates Dr. D interrupting our groove.

I open my legs and press my hand to T's hip, urging him to move closer. He rises above me and shuffles to lie between my spread legs, with his cock at my entrance.

"You've both been tested with no evidence of STDs. Ms. K's birth-control levels are adequate to prevent pregnancy, so we will skip a condom today. Removing that takes away one variable to explain why you both might have difficulty finding release during sex." Dr. D drones on, but neither T nor I are listening because he's kissing me again and I'm guiding him into my entrance.

He pushes in, just the tip, and we both cry out. Even though I'm wet, I've always been tight and he's big, so it takes a few minutes of T pressing in, waiting for me to stretch, and then repeating the process. I murmur encouragingly the entire time, telling him that I'm okay, that I want him inside of me, that he feels so damn good. I always say these things to the men I sleep with, and most of the time they're lies, but this time I'm being honest. Because I do want him in me, and it does feel *so* fucking good.

Finally, after several painstaking minutes, he's all the way in, nice and deep. I'm full of him. I take a second to marvel at how well he fits. T lifts his lips from mine and kisses down my neck as he starts to move. I tilt my chin to give him better access as my pelvis lifts up to match the motion of his hips. T's moving faster now. He pulls almost all the way out and then slams back in, his breath sputtering against my neck, bursts of warm air mingled with groans and sighs.

There's a tightening in my core, a warmth deep inside that I know from masturbating means an orgasm is building.

This is it! I think. *I'm going to come!*

T's movements grow choppy and uncoordinated. His eyes squeeze shut, and the muscles of his neck strain.

We're going to come together!

Joy surges through me. I can't believe it's this easy. That knot winds tighter in me, my hands claw his back, and then...nothing. The feeling doesn't disappear in a puff of smoke—it fades, growing slowly fainter and fainter until I can't sense it at all. I hold out hope that even if it doesn't happen for me, at least T will find release, but the same thing happens to him. His movements slow, become more erratic, like he's trying to discover just the right angle or the right pace to get us off.

Finally, he collapses on me, sweaty and out of breath. "I'm sorry," he mumbles into my collarbone. "I couldn't do it." There's despair in those words, with a healthy dose of shame and self-loathing.

I run my hands over his back, tracing soothing patterns into his skin. "It's okay. I couldn't either." Shadows that haunt the corners of my mind creep forward to tell me that I'm a failure. That it's because I'm not pretty enough, thin enough, good enough. That's why I can't do this simple task, something everyone else can accomplish with little effort.

Chapter Seven

"Don't be discouraged," Dr. D says, in what is probably a normal voice, but to my depressed ears sounds overly enthusiastic. "Most couples require several times before they achieve success."

T groans into my chest, not the seductive noises he made earlier, but a sound of annoyance, of defeat.

Unfazed, Dr. D. continues, "In the personality tests you completed, both of you measure strongly as people pleasers, willing to sacrifice yourself for others. This is a common trait we see in patients with your particular challenge. I suspect you both have trouble communicating your desires to your partners and, thus, are often left unsatisfied."

Those words strike *way* too close to home for me. Judging by the exaggerated flinch T just gave, he feels the same.

"I'd like to bolster your interpersonal communication skills in this area by performing an exercise. Would the two of you be open to that?"

Silent nods from T and myself.

"Wonderful!" says Dr. D. "Please, both of you lie on the bed and face each other."

We shuffle ourselves until I have my head on one pillow and T has the other. This is such an intimate position, lying here with no choice but to stare into T's eyes, which are fixed on me, intense and unblinking. A strange kind of shyness settles over me, prickling at my skin. I carefully tuck the sheet under my arm, making sure it covers my chest. T mirrors me, pulling the blanket up as well.

"Good. Good," calls out Dr. D. "Now, without looking away I want you to take turns telling the other person one sexual act you would like performed on you. Please be as detailed, as explicit, as possible."

T's eyes widen at that, at the same time that my stomach drops. I'm not good at this, at articulating my thoughts, especially when it comes to something so vulnerable.

"Well?" prompts Dr. D after a beat of drawn-out silence.

Nothing from us. We're playing a silent game of chicken, daring the other to go first with our eyes.

Dr. D lets out an exasperated sigh. "T. Why don't you start?"

T opens his mouth like he wants to protest, but he snaps it shut. His eyes dart away, and he stutters out, "Uh...I like it when I—I'm," he winces, squishing his face together. Then, super-fast, he rushes out, "on the bottom."

"Yes," says Dr. D patiently. "Tell us some more. Why, exactly, do you enjoy that?"

T grimaces, like this conversation is causing him physical pain. "I don't know. I just do."

"There's always a reason. Look deeper," says Dr. D.

I have to give the doctor credit. He's persistent, not falling for T's stonewalling.

T bites his lip. "I guess it's because I'm tired of being in charge. Of always having to think ahead, take control." He looks at me, his expression earnest. "It's not that I'm lazy. I won't lie there and make you do all the work. It's just that sometimes I want to shut my brain off. Let someone else take the lead. That way, I don't have to overthink every movement. I don't have to wonder if I'm going too fast, too slow, too hard, too soft. It takes the pressure off." He hesitates. "Does that make sense?"

I nod, a smile pulling at the corners of my lips.

T notices. "What? Is that funny?" His jaw tenses like he's bracing for judgment.

A tiny giggle escapes. "It's only funny because I *love* to be on top. I was going to say that as *my* answer."

"No way! You do?" His face brightens, splits into a brilliant smile, then slowly fades. "Or are you just saying that so you don't have to come up with something original?" he asks, his voice heavy with suspicion.

I roll my eyes, annoyed he's not taking my word for it. "*Really*? You think I'd lie about *that*?"

T drops his gaze. A guilty flush climbs his neck as he mumbles, "Sorry."

"Please elaborate, K," breaks in Dr. D. I look at the mirror, almost expecting to see him, but only my reflection stares back. "Why do you prefer that position over others?"

"Well, I like it for all the same reasons you don't," I tell T. "*I* want to be in charge. That way no one can hurt me. No one can go too hard or too fast. See? Like you, but the opposite."

A shadow moves over T's face. "Why would you be hurt? It's sex. You shouldn't worry about that."

For a minute, I want to snap at him, tell him to stop being so ignorant. Of course you can be hurt during sex. You can be hurt any time you open up to another person. Not everyone is gentle. Not every touch feels good. Experience has taught me that lesson, many times over.

I don't tell him any of that. It's too personal to share with this stranger, even if I did just have him inside me. Instead, I pull the covers higher, up to my neck. "I like that *I* get to make the call, that's all."

T watches me for a long moment, like he's searching for something just out of reach.

"Great," Dr. D says, his voice bright, almost cheerful. "Since you're both in agreement, let's go ahead and try that position."

I tense, my fingers tightening on the sheets.

"But this time," he continues, "I want to hear you communicate. No holding back. No worrying that you're being too demanding. I want full honesty."

T shifts beside me. "Like...out loud?"

Dr. D chuckles. "Yes, out loud." A pause. "I need to hear exactly what you want. Every detail. Every command."

A shiver of dread runs through me. I'm not sure I can do this. Having sex with a stranger is one thing. Having to *talk* my way through it is another.

T scoots closer, reaching for me under the sheets. "What—where do you want me to touch you?" he asks in a low, whispery voice.

"I—um—" The words stick in my throat, refusing to come out.

"How about between your legs?" T supplies helpfully.

I nod, grateful he came to my rescue.

"Words, please," Dr. D. commands loudly. I jump, guiltily, like I got caught cheating on my homework assignment.

"I want you to stroke my—my clit. Do it until I'm wet, dripping for you," I whisper, unable to look T in the eye, but I hear it. The way he gusts out a whispered *fuck* that's full of desire.

"That was hot," T says, as his fingers land exactly where I told them to go.

I moan, throwing my head back. T's right there, licking and kissing my neck, making butterflies swoop low in my stomach.

"Tell T how that feels," Dr. D instructs, but I barely hear him because T is matching the roll of my hips perfectly.

"Good," I groan out.

"More detailed, please," Dr. D corrects.

"It feels—it feels..."

Work, brain. Work.

"It feels like you're made of lightning, T, and you're electrocuting me, but in a good way."

Oh, my God. I internally wince.

My brain is so weird.

T snickers. "That was descriptive."

"What do you want T to do next?" Dr. D's voice is clinical, detached.

I'm panting, my breath coming in quick, short bursts. "I w—want him—to put his fingers in me, but don't stop touching my clit. I want him to flick it, rub it harder."

"Jesus," T growls out. He's practically salivating next to me. He's quick to comply with my demands.

I cry out when he penetrates me with not just one but two fingers. The stretch of it is delicious.

"Okay, T," interrupts Dr. D. "It's your turn. What would you like right now?"

T doesn't even hesitate. His voice hoarse, he says, "I want to fuck her. With her on top, riding me."

Those words send arousal stabbing into me, low in my belly, so sharp it almost hurts. "Yes," I say. "I want that, too."

We scramble, tripping over each other, as T shifts onto his back and I rise above him. I fling my leg over him, straddling his erection, which stands tall, pointing straight up to the ceiling. I sink down on him with a sigh, taking him slowly, inch by inch. He's already bucking by the time I reach the bottom. T digs his fingers into my hips. With gentle pressure, he guides me up and down.

"Communicate, T. What do you want?" Dr. D's voice is a drone in the background.

"I want to fuck K hard and fast," T grits out.

"Hey!" I tease, grinning down at him. "You said *I* was the one in charge." I give him a playful smack on the shoulder.

He pauses at that. Chuckling, T smiles up at me in an open, amused way, so disarming with his cheeks tinged pink, his hair tousled, his eyes glazed with lust, and—*damn*—if he's not the most beautiful thing I've ever seen.

"Fucking with me, while you're fucking me," he murmurs lazily, his eyes half-lidded, as he resumes the pump of his hips. "I like it, K."

Warmth bubbles up, but not from my core—*no*—this is in my chest. Affection, not just attraction. The last emotion I ever thought I'd feel in this cold, white room. Stunned, I halt mid-thrust. T grips me harder, yanks me down, and we both groan.

"I can't wait to make you come, K." Apparently, he's in a talking mood now. His hands urge me on, faster and faster, building the friction between us. "It's going to feel so good. It's going to *be* so good to watch you unravel on my cock."

His words travel straight to my core, slickening it, making it ache for him. It occurs to me that he's not just thinking about his pleasure, but about *mine*. Before I almost saw him as my opponent. Like we were on opposite sides of a chess board, but now I see we're playing on the same side. If I win, he wins, and vice versa.

What happens when you put two people pleasers together?

They want to please each other.

That might not be a bad thing.

There's the crackle of the microphone turning on, but before Dr. D can speak, T waves his hand, a shooing motion to the mirror, like Dr. D is a pest right now.

"I know, I know. Tell her what I want." T beats Dr. D to the punch. His eyes are glued to my breasts, which sway with each thrust. In a calm, clear voice, he says, "K, I want to suck on your tits while you bounce on my dick until we both come screaming."

Wow. That was...wow.

T sits up, wrapping his arms around my back, and folds me close to him. He takes my breast into his mouth, sucking on my nipple, swirling his tongue over the tip, while I move up and down on his shaft. The sensation of his warm, wet mouth on my breast and his dick in my pussy combine into one large pulse of desire. I wind my arms around his head and hold him to me.

"Oh, yes," I gasp. Gathering the things we learned about communication, I tell T, "I want you to squeeze my other breast. Hard."

"Mmm." He nuzzles the breast he's been working on, then goes back to sucking on it while his other hand comes to clasp the unoccupied one. A pinch to that nipple turns me on even more. We move together, our hands growing bolder, our voices steadier. The more we talk, the easier it gets. A whispered request. A quiet moan in response.

It's working. *God*, it feels like it's actually working. For a moment, I forget about Dr. D, forget about the sterile walls, the lack of windows, and the clinical lights glowing dimly above us. It's just T and me, warmth spreading between us like an ember catching flame.

T moves his lips from my breast to my shoulder, his breath hot against my skin. "That good?" he murmurs. His fingers are back on my clit, just like I told him.

"Yeah," I whisper, almost surprised by how much I mean it. "Really good."

We keep going, following the rhythm we've fallen into, and I'm almost there. *Almost*. But then—

Something shifts.

T changes the angle, just slightly, and suddenly the heat fizzles. I try to ignore it, try to focus on the way his hands feel on me, but the moment is slipping, like trying to hold onto water. I grab for that feeling once more, that slow climb to orgasm, but my hands come up empty.

T's breathing changes too. Hesitates. Quiets.

The pressure that was building between us fades. When T lets out a deep sigh, I know he feels it too.

Finally, we slow down. He presses his forehead to my chest, his breath shaky. "It's not working, is it?"

I want to lie to him, to spare him, to keep this fragile thing we almost had from falling to pieces completely. But this exercise was all about communication, so I force myself to shake my head. "I'm sorry."

T's body stiffens. His fingers go slack, fall away from my body and into his lap.

I pull off of him, exhausted, and collapse onto my back, draping a hand over my eyes.

Neither of us speaks. The room is too quiet. The absence of our gasping breaths makes the silence oppressive. I turn my head, searching his expression. T stares at the ceiling, his jaw clenched, his lips parted like he wants to say something but doesn't know how. A muscle in his cheek ticks.

I reach for him, but my hand stalls inches from his skin.

When he doesn't look at me, I let my hand fall away.

That's when I hear it—his small, barely-there whisper of defeat.

"*Shit.*"

Chapter Eight

"Why don't we try it from behind?" Dr. D. suggests. T lifts his head and meets my eyes. I see the reflection of my own misery.

"Fine," T grumbles.

I flip over like a pancake and rise to my hands and knees. A glance over my shoulder shows T moving into position behind me. Luckily, he's still hard and I'm still wet so he's able to slide into me without too much fuss. He places his hands on my hips and uses them to guide me, pulling me back to him and then pushing me away. He thrusts into me slowly, like he's building his strength back up. It feels good, but not great, definitely not enough to get me to the big O.

T leans forward, folding himself over so his chest is to my back. He brings his hands around and uses one to anchor himself to my hip. The other he uses to stroke my clit, which is swollen and sensitive.

This...this feels good...like *really* good.

"Yes," I moan, the sound low as if it's being ripped out of my throat. "Right there. Don't stop."

T kisses my back. He pushes his dick in and out, all the while rubbing my clit to the same fast pace. It feels good, *he* feels good, but I can't tell if this is affecting him the way it is me. I keep looking back, noting how he's too in control, with his eyes locked on me like he's memorizing every expression on my face, every sound I make.

Worried about T and his need for pleasure, I slow down. "Is...is it not okay for you? You can do other things if you need," I offer. "You can hit me, pull my hair, call me names."

T rears back like I just pulled a gun on him. "Jesus!" he yells, his face twisted with horror. "Why the fuck would I do that?"

Shame marks my skin scarlet. I don't have to see to know I'm burning up with embarrassment.

"Some guys like it," I answer defensively.

"Who?" he demands. He's still buried in me but frozen in place like he can't have this conversation and fuck me at the same time.

I hang my head low. "Guys," I mumble, wishing I'd never brought it up.

"Guys you've been with? You let them do those things to you?"

Mute, unable to look him in the eye, I nod.

"Did you like them, those things?"

I shake my head, burning tears pricking the back of my eyes, as I remember all the demeaning and sometimes horrific things I've let men do to me. I sniffle but don't cry. I never let them see me cry. It's a rule I have. One I never break.

A quick glance shows that T's brows have knitted together. He's frowning. His grip on me tightens as he struggles to understand.

"Why, K? Why would you let them?"

My voice is husky, thick with the tears I swallow down but don't let fall. "I thought maybe the reason I couldn't come was because I hadn't tried enough things, like different ways to have sex. I thought if I pushed my boundaries, tried to have rougher sex, dirtier sex, I'd find a way."

"It didn't work?"

"I'm here, so—no. It didn't."

"Oh." T falls silent, but not an empty silence, one that's full of questions, all of which I'm not ready to answer. I've left that part of my life behind, and I have no desire to revisit it.

"It's nothing, really. I don't do that anymore. Can we just drop it?" I cast a pleading glance at him.

T straightens, his mouth still downturned. He clears his throat. "Um, okay—sure." He runs his hand over my back. "I like your tattoos," he says, and I'm so grateful for his tactful change of subject that the urge to cry hits me again.

I battle it down and tell him a choked, "Thanks."

"I wish you could tell me what they all mean." He traces the ink on my back with his finger, like a blind person reading Braille. "But I guess we don't have time for that, do we?"

Longing washes over me as my imagination takes over. A lifetime flashes by in a second. I picture T and me on a date, laughing at an outdoor restaurant. We're at the movies, sharing a bucket of popcorn. We're walking through a garden, lounging on a beach, traveling in a car, an airplane, a boat. He's down on one knee, we walk down the aisle, a baby with warm brown eyes gurgles in my arms.

Stop it! I scream at my stupid, idiotic, messed-up brain. He's already done those things with someone else—his *wife*. The relationship he's trying to fix. Good grief! What the fuck is wrong with me? I've never been good at this—separating sex and love. This is the reason I've made so many poor choices in men, why I've been left heartbroken over and over by guys whose only goal was to get in my pants.

He's here to fuck you, not love you, you moron.

Chapter Nine

Dr. D chooses this moment to intervene. "I'd like you to resume intercourse now," he says in his stiff, formal way. I picture him as old, with bushy white eyebrows and thick black glasses. "T, continue to stimulate her clitoris while you have sex. K said in her survey that she rarely comes without it."

It shouldn't be embarrassing that the doctor revealed that intimate detail, especially since T's literally buried inside me, yet somehow…it is. I stiffen, my thoughts elsewhere. I'm barely aware that T is still with me, not until he presses his lips to my back and asks, "You ready?"

He waits for me to nod, then wraps his arm back around me. His fingers find my clit easily this time, like he's learning my body. He circles soft, then hard, then soft again.

It takes a few minutes for me to calm down enough to enjoy it, to let the pleasure radiate from his touch to the rest of my body, but he doesn't stop or complain. He stays at it, steadfast. Stroking, rubbing, until my arousal slickens his hand and his cock.

He finally starts to move his hips. Long slow draws out and quick hard shoves in. Hand on my clit. Cock in my pussy. I can feel when he gets out of his head enough to focus on his own pleasure. He groans, panting, loses the controlled way he was fucking me and moves into a more frantic, irregular rhythm.

"Oh, fuck," he grits out, breathing hard. "You feel so fucking good. This is it—it's going to work."

I push back against him, matching his movements, urging him on with the motion of my hips. "Yes, yes," I chant. "It's going to work." There it is again, that coiling sensation. The rising tension of an impending orgasm. My toes curl, my legs and arms shake. I cry out, "Faster!"

He obliges, rapidly picking up his speed. "Come on, K. You can do it."

Usually, during sex, I think about the guy. Wonder if he's enjoying himself and attempt to figure out the best way to get him off. Not this time. This time I'm selfish. I narrow my focus to the sensation of T's skin on mine. Of his dick filling up my needy pussy. The tension in my body heightens to the point that it's almost painful. My arms shake from holding myself up. My back spasms. Pleasure grows deep in my low stomach. It rises and rises and rises and then…I lose it. That sensation of bliss. It escapes from my grasp like a balloon handed to a toddler. I can almost see it float away from me.

T loses it at the same time. He stutters, slows down, and swears a muttered curse.

I collapse forward, pulling myself off T's cock in the process, and break my only rule. I burst into tears. Heartbroken by my failure and ashamed of my weakness, I bury my head in the pillow to hide.

T's there immediately. He pulls me out and drags me around so I'm on my back. He runs his hands over me, babbling, "Oh my God, K. Are you okay? Did I hurt you? Did something happen? Fuck. I should've slowed down, been gentler. I'm so sorry. I just wanted to get you there. I thought you were liking it." His voice hitches, breaks, like he's on the verge of tears as well.

"I'm sorry. I fucked up."

He buries his head in my chest, and I wrap my arms around him. "No," I sob, pulling him close. I'm ugly crying now, the kind with snot and puffy eyes where you end up congested for the rest of the day.

"It's not your fault. It's mine. *I'm* the screw-up."

T lifts his head, his eyes shiny. "No, you're *not*," he says fiercely, his mouth drawn. "You are *not* a screw-up. I don't want to hear you say that ever again!"

"I am, though," I argue, hiccupping on my tears, choking on them, drowning as the enormity of my loss hits me. "I'm never going to have a normal sex life. Never going to know what it feels like to come in someone's arms. I'm a fuck-up. Who will ever want me? Someone broken like me?"

Tenderly, with the pad of his thumb, T brushes away my tears. He kisses them away. "That's not true. You're not broken. You're beautiful and strong."

I whip my head from side to side, shaking it. "*No*. I'm not. I'm weak and boring and stupid. So dumb to have gotten my hopes up. To believe something this deranged might actually work."

"Hey, now," he chides. "We're not giving up yet. There's still hope."

My lower lip juts out. Eyes bleary with tears, I stubbornly tell him, "There's *not*. We tried, and we failed. It's probably all my fault. Maybe if you were paired with someone better, you would've had a chance. Sorry you got stuck with me." I squeeze my eyes shut, unable to look at him.

T kisses my closed eyelids. He chases my tears with his tongue and lips. "There's no one else. No one I'd rather be here with than you, K. I was so fucking scared when I walked in here. Seriously, I was one minute away from chickening out, calling the entire thing off. Do you know what made me change my mind?"

"No," I say, still crying. "I have no idea."

"You," T says simply, like I'm the answer to every question. "I saw you when I walked through that door, and all I could think was, 'wow.' You're so gorgeous. Totally out of my league. When you started to talk, I saw that not only are you beautiful, but you're also whip smart. You're feisty and brave and I thought that even though I'm a wimp, you're not, so I knew we'd be okay. That no matter how this turns out, I've already won because I got to meet you and then to be able to do this with you, to make love to you?" His voice goes high, incredulous, as he stares down at me and completes his thought, "Well, that's just icing on the cake. Especially for a guy like me, who is used to being a disappointment." He looks away, his throat working.

"Hey," I say, trying to get his attention back. "You're never a disappointment to me, even if this doesn't work. Okay?"

A sorrowful nod from him.

"Ugh!" I clap my hands over my eyes. "But *why* isn't it working? I don't understand. Why can't we do it?" I ask, pleading, as tears rain down my cheeks.

T stares down at me, sadness in the droop of his head, like it's too heavy. His shoulders sag, and his breath stutters. "I don't know. Just—please don't cry. You're breaking my fucking heart."

His voice is rough, almost desperate. "Tell me what to do. What can I do to make this better?"

I swallow hard. "Hold me for now," I whisper. "I don't need you to fix me. Just hold me."

Something in him softens. Without a word, he rolls onto his back and pulls me into him, pressing me against his chest. I wrap my arms around him and bury my face in the curve of his neck, breathing him in, taking comfort in his warmth, the slow rise and fall of his ribs beneath my palm.

Silence stretches between us, thick and heavy.

I close my eyes and listen to the quiet, absorbing the way our bodies fit together so perfectly. For a moment, I let myself believe that I could stay here, like this, forever.

T's hand moves slowly, absently, tracing circles against my back. I feel his chest rise with a breath, then still. Like he's about to say something, but he holds it back.

Minutes pass. Maybe hours.

Finally, he exhales. "Something's missing."

Chapter Ten

"What? What's missing?" I ask, desperate to find a solution to our problem.

"I think—" He pauses, stares off into the distance. "I think it's love. That's what we're missing."

I snort a bitter laugh. "Kinda hard to fall in love, given these circumstances. Besides, you're already in love, with your wife."

"I used to think I was in love with her. Now, I'm not sure, not even sure I know what love is." T hesitates, rubbing his palm over his jaw. "I don't even know why I'm doing this anymore," he admits. "It started for her. To prove I was worth staying for. But now..." His eyes flick to mine. "Now, I don't know if I want to be fixed for her. I think I want to be fixed for me."

His gaze finds mine, something fragile and real flickering there. "And I want *you* to feel fixed too, for yourself."

My heart melts at that, his kindness. How he's not just thinking about himself in this moment, but about me as well. We gaze at each other, and I feel a connection between us solidify. It hums with life, impossible but undeniable. It's been growing since we first touched. Since he first whispered my name. Since I first let him in.

T hesitates, like he's fighting something inside himself. "I know this isn't forever. I understand we just met and don't really know each other, but I have feelings for you. They probably won't last past today, and normally I'd ignore them until they went away, but what if *that's* the thing we need? What if—just for now—I could love you, and you loved me back? Not as a promise. Not as a lie. Just as…this. What we are, here in this room. Two people searching for something they've never been given. Something we have to fight for—together."

A lump rises in my throat. My mind protests, tells me this is reckless, that I should guard myself. But my body, my heart, they already know the answer. It was in my daydream, with the dates and the proposal, the baby. It's true, I don't know him at all, yet somehow I do. This experience has been so outside the realm of normal that my emotions have snowballed quickly, coalesced into something that feels very much like love.

He says it hesitantly, like he's testing out the words. "I love you, K." Another kiss to my forehead, so tender and sweet. "It's not forever, not meant to last, but it's real. It's here inside of me. I can't explain it. I don't want to. Let's just let it be."

It's been years since I was loved, so long ago that I don't remember what it feels like. I've been admired, lusted after, used, and thrown away, but never loved. I let his words sink into me, absorb them through my skin and into my soul.

"I love you too." I say it with more confidence than T did, maybe because my feelings are clearer, less muddled from being attached to someone else. I lift my hand and skim it along his cheek. "Just for now, and that's okay. It's crazy, though, isn't it? To care about you this quickly?"

He dips his head, touches his forehead to mine. "This whole thing is crazy—doesn't make it any less real."

His mouth finds mine, and I let myself sink into it, let myself feel it, all of it.

The tenderness. The hunger. The warmth of his hands and the steady strength of his body.

The way he makes me feel like I matter.

His lips are salty from my tears. His tongue brushes mine, and the air around us shifts, becomes charged and electric. His hands slide down my body, stroking, soothing.

"Let me love you, just for now." His voice catches on the words.

"Yes," I whisper back. "Love me."

He keeps on kissing me, lazy and slow. Like we have the entire day, a lifetime, to explore this new thing between us. I run my hands up and down his back, marveling at the solidness of him, at how his body is hard but his heart is soft.

His hand dips between my legs, and a gasp spills from my lips and colors explode behind my eyelids. I'm soaked down there, so ready for him, more than I've ever been. We shift together, my thighs parting like an invitation, my body welcoming his. When he slides inside, a long, shuddering breath leaves him, like he's just come home.

He makes love to me the same way he kissed me, slow and sweet, as if he wants to savor it, make it last. Each movement is deliberate yet delicate, like I matter, as if he wants to treat me gently. Every few minutes, he sends me a tender glance, checking to see if I'm still with him, if I'm okay.

This time there's no pressure. No urgency. I'm not thinking about how to please him or how to force my body to respond. I'm not second-guessing myself or overanalyzing every touch, every breath, every shift between us.

Instead, I think about the way he described me as beautiful, smart, and brave. Words I've never truly heard, not when they were spoken by others, not even when I tried to tell them to myself. But when T said them, they felt different. Like he meant them.

"Love you," he repeats into my skin, my hair, and for the first time I don't question it. I just let myself believe that I'm the person he described.

Someone worth loving.

"Love you," I sigh back, soaking in the sight and sound of him. Mint and sunshine and tan skin that's rough in all the right places.

T hums, gives me a small smile. "This feels good, K. I want to stay in you forever."

Forever.

What a beautiful word. It seems like something I should pay attention to, analyze, fear.

But I don't.

Because right now, there's only this. The slick slide of his body against mine, the pressure building between us. The heat, the need. The way my pulse pounds in my ears as my body tightens around him.

I don't have to think. Don't have to worry about what happens when this is over.

I just let go.

"So good," I slur, my mind consumed by the fire that's building deep inside me, lit by T's words of love, the honeyed sensation of him moving in and out slow as molasses but gaining speed now.

His fingers stroke between my legs, circling, pressing, teasing. "Tell me what you want."

I whimper, twisting against him, my body surging into his touch. Then I remember our lesson on communication. "I need you to touch my clit."

He smiles at me, like he's proud, then brings his hand between us to flick my clit, sending an ache spiking through my body.

"Oh God," I pant. "Yes."

His pace quickens, his lips trailing down my throat.

It's happening—finally, finally happening.

"Shit," he gets out. "It's—you're incredible, so beautiful." He moves faster, his hip bones dancing under my fingers. T swears, driving into me hard, over and over. "I'm getting close."

Tears leak out of the corner of my eyes as my muscles clench, tighten, until I'm shaking. "Me too." This is it, the same sensation when I pleasure myself, right before I come. That feeling of careening toward the edge of a cliff, about to fall off the precipice.

"Say it," T demands, his eyes squeezed tight, his skin flushed. "Say you love me. Come with me. We do this together."

"Together. I'm coming, T. It's happening. I love you so fucking much!" The last word leaves my mouth as the orgasm hits me, a tidal wave that drags me under the water, drowning me with sensation. I'm pulsating, quivering, crying out as I lose myself in it.

"Yes. Do it. Love you." T lets go as well. With a hoarse groan, he gives one, then two more jerks and comes shuddering deep inside me, so hard I feel him fill me up.

Our orgasms seem to go on for a long time, both of us trembling with shivers of pleasure that wrack our bodies.

Finally, he softens and pulls out, leaving a rush of warmth that drips down my thighs. He rolls onto his back, pulling me along with him so I'm draped over his chest with my ear over his heart. I take comfort from the sound, that steady lub-dub.

Chapter Eleven

"We did it!" T says into my hair, exultant. "I can't believe it."

I turn my head toward him and smile as wide as my cheeks will go. "We did."

Eyes bright, he grins at me. "I've got it now. I see what I need to do. It's the love, K. I just need to remember the love. To focus on that and the rest will follow."

His excitement is infectious. I can't help but grin back. My body is sore, spent, but underneath the exhaustion, something inside me clicks into place. I look inward, toward where pleasure finally let me in, and I realize he's right. The door to my release opened with love.

But not his.

Mine.

My breath catches as the truth unfurls inside me. It wasn't his love that gave me permission to let go. It was the love I found for myself.

I swallow hard. "Love," I whisper. "That's the key. Oh! And communication."

"And trust." He looks at me, his eyes glowing. "I trust you, K."

My chest constricts, but not in a bad way. It's different this time. Safer. Realer.

"Me, too." I snuggle closer and break into a giggle. "We sound like a Hallmark card."

He laughs with me. "I know, and that's okay."

I shift, tilting my head up so I can see him better, and he mirrors the movement, grinning down at me. The space between us hums, something new and unspoken hanging in the air. Slowly, he leans in, his lips pursed like he's going to kiss me—

Dr. D's voice cuts through the moment. "Excellent job, T and K! Really good work. I couldn't be happier with your results today. I'm confident you'll be able to reproduce this with your current and future partners now that you've had this breakthrough."

Current partner.

His wife.

T freezes, his lips so close to mine I can feel the warm exhale of his breath. Then he backs up. He puts his head on the pillow and stares at the ceiling, his face—usually so animated—wiped clean. A tense silence descends. In it I hear the echoes of our whispered I love you's. The words I clung to, that I let myself believe. But now, in the cold light of reality, they don't sound romantic.

They sound like betrayal.

My stomach twists. Dr. D said his wife would be okay with this, but would she really? Would I be okay if our roles were reversed? Sure, I can justify it with the fact that they're separated, maybe headed for a divorce, but *I* can't be the one to force that decision. I don't want the blame for their failed marriage.

Scrambling, I push off T and sit up to comb my fingers through the snarls of my tangled hair. I let the strands fall like a curtain, shielding me.

"You'll receive a follow-up questionnaire," Dr. D continues. Since he's not in the room, maybe he doesn't understand how the temperature just plummeted twenty degrees. "I'll send my bill to the email addresses you provided earlier. Just a hundred dollars. A very reasonable fee."

The lights turn up, flooding the room with clinical brightness. I hiss through my teeth, blinded by the sterile glare.

Reality punches its way to the front of my post-orgasm–addled brain, and it's not pretty. This isn't love. This was a mistake. I need to remember that it's a business transaction, nothing more. All parties got what they came for, and now there's no reason to linger. I shuffle off the bed and separate my clothing from T's. My shirt is inside out. His pants button is somehow caught in my fishnet stockings. Painstakingly, with numb fingers, I free it, then toss T's clothing onto the bed where he still lays, frozen like a statue, naked as the day he was born.

"Here you go," I say, my tone sharper than I intended as I avert my gaze from his near-perfect body. I'm not sure how to handle this. How to come down from this high without feeling like I just went skydiving but my parachute never opened.

The pants hit T in the chest, and he flinches. I watch out of the corner of my eye, not brave enough to stare at him head on in these harsh conditions.

"Thanks," he mumbles. He turns away from me as he dresses, which shouldn't matter, I tell myself it doesn't, but in reality it cuts deep, like he just plunged a knife into my heart. After all that intimacy, now I'm back to being a stranger, not allowed to see him naked.

Chapter Twelve

Once he's fully clothed, T comes to me with his hands shoved deep in his pockets, as if he's hiding them. I wonder what they would do if he released them. Would they reach for me? Touch me? Hug me?

I'll never know. There's a distance between us, a frigid tundra colder than the air conditioning that blasts over my head.

"Well, uh, thanks," he says, his eyes focused on something over my shoulder. I glance behind to see what has him so fascinated but there's nothing, just emptiness.

I force my arms to stay at my sides. I will *not* reach for him. I refuse to be the only one reaching.

"Yeah." My voice has lost all inflection. Something in me is dying a slow, tortuous death. "You too. Thanks."

"Well..." He rocks on his heels, seemingly at war with himself. "I'm not sure what to say. My wife—ex—whatever. I promised her I'd try, and I feel like I should let her know what's happened. That I can do it now."

His throat works. His jaw flexes. His voice is careful, deliberate. Like he's trying to convince himself as much as me.

"We've been together a long time," he continues. "I can't just throw that away." A pause. "That makes sense, right?"

A cruel, awful part of me wants to scream *no* at him. No, it doesn't make sense. That same part wants to say that I don't care about his promises or his obligations. That if he chooses to walk away from me, he's a coward.

But that would be a lie. Because I *do* understand.

It makes perfect sense. Of course he has to try.

And the saddest part? If I were in his shoes, I'd make the same choice.

Wouldn't I?

He watches me carefully, the corners of his mouth pulling downward. "Are you...gonna be okay?"

What am I supposed to say to that?

No, actually, I'm going to shatter into a million pieces. You're about to walk out that door and take something from me that I can't name but know I'll never get back.

Or worse—should I ask him to choose *me*?

Demand he throw away a lifetime for someone he just met?

I can't do that.

I won't stand in the way of his happiness.

I do what I always do. I take the hit, let it carve into me like a blade, let the pain lodge itself so deep it'll take years to dig out.

I pull the same old, tired armor over my heart. I force my lips into the best fake smile I've got, the one I've been perfecting for years, and pitch my voice high and bright.

"I'm great."

Lie.

As if we were strangers—which, I remind myself, we are—I say, "It was nice to meet you."

He searches me, his gaze heavy with suspicion. As much as I'm hurting right now, I just want this to be over. To rip off the Band-Aid and bleed out somewhere else. Anywhere but here. The back of my nose stings with unshed tears, but I already broke my rule once and look where it got me. I won't make that mistake again.

I stare at him without blinking, silently projecting the message of *I don't care. I'm fine. You didn't hurt me.*

"Okay…" He hesitates. The silence stretches out painfully long. "I guess, thanks again and good luck."

Good luck.

Like this was some kind of job interview. As if we hadn't just laid each other bare, held each other, whispered that we love each other.

Like none of it meant anything.

"You too!" I say, forcing cheer into my voice. I even wave. As if he's stepping onto the *Titanic* and I'm standing on the dock, sending him off with a big, bright bon voyage smile.

His face twists like he's in physical pain. It pinches with discomfort, maybe even disappointment, then evens out, the expression fleeting—gone in a second.

He gives one sharp nod.

Then he turns.

And walks out the door.

It hasn't even swung shut before I crumple to my knees, sobbing onto my bent forearms. Nausea rises in me. The room spins.

When Dr. D speaks, I want to scream, to shatter the window that separates us so I can strangle him with my bare hands. I'm unable to take responsibility, too busy wallowing in my misery, so I put the blame on him, on T.

"This is normal, Kristi," he says. "All patients get attached. It's part of the process."

"He didn't," I sob. "T wasn't attached. He just walked away like it was no big deal."

"It's just as hard on him as it is on you." The doctor's voice is surprisingly gentle. "He handles his pain differently, that's all."

"No," I say stubbornly. My shadows are back, whispering, pointing out all my flaws. "He didn't care. It was all a lie. He just needed to fuck me so he could get over his problem. Once it was solved, you saw what happened—how quickly he ran out of here, back to her."

I take in a shuddering breath and scream at the mirror, "You shouldn't mess with people's feelings like this. It's fucked up!"

"But you got what you wanted, right?" the voice says.

Did I? Get what I wanted?

Nothing is clear to me right now. I'm too overwhelmed. Too gutted to think rationally. Like an overstimulated teenager, I scream, "I hate you!" and run from the room, out into the street.

The moment I push through the doors, it's like stepping onto another planet. The world is too bright, too *alive*. Sunlight slants between scattered clouds. Car horns blare. Voices rise and fall in easy conversation. A gust of air carries the smell of the city—sweat, hot pavement, the sewer beneath my feet.

I stumble forward, vision swimming, dodging pedestrians who shoot me wary glances. Two blocks. That's as far as I get before my body gives out. My knees buckle, and I sink to the sidewalk, back against a brick wall, gasping for breath.

No one stops. No one asks if I'm okay. And I'm grateful for it. The best—and worst—part of living in New York.

A sob claws its way up my throat. I clap my hands over my ears, desperate to shut it all out, but it's useless. His words are still there. Replaying in my head, over and over.

"I love you."

I can't believe I listened.

Let myself hope.
Fucking liar.
No one loves me.
Least of all myself.

Chapter Thirteen

Epilogue

One year later

The subway train's arrival is announced first by a gust of wind, warm and smelling of the swamp this city is built on. Then there's the squealing of metal wheels as it brakes. Finally, the train itself, tagged with layers of graffiti, lumbers into view. The double doors whoosh open, and strangers pile in. I shift my feet, shuffling in along with the nameless crowd. There are no seats available, and even if there were I wouldn't take them. I'm young and healthy. There's no reason for me to sit, not when other people need it more.

The doors close, and everyone clusters tightly together, a shifting mass of humanity. Since I'm shorter than average, I'm always at a disadvantage. The looped straps that hang overhead, the ones most people hold onto, are too high unless I'm on my toes. I reach for one now but miss it by a centimeter at the same moment that the train lurches into motion. Off balance, I fall backward with my arms windmilling, smacking people as I go down. I brace for the humiliation of hitting the dirty floor, but before that happens someone yells out a surprised, "Whoa!" Strong arms catch me, then right me, setting me gently on my feet.

I open my mouth to say thank you just as the scent of mint hits my nose. My breath catches. My brain rewinds.

A white room.

Tangled sheets.

I turn sharply, my pulse hammering, and suddenly—he's there before me. Not a memory, like the one I've replayed so many times. The real man, flesh and blood, tall and brown-haired. Warm brown eyes flung wide, staring at me like I'm a dream he just woke up from.

"K?" he breathes, searching my face. "Is that you?"

My hand flies up to pat my hair, purple now, but it doesn't matter. He knows me. "Y—yes? T?"

His hands haven't let go from catching me. They stay on my hips, large and warm. He tightens them, steadies me, because I've begun to wobble. I want to blame it on the motion of the train, but deep down, I know better.

Be normal. Act normal.

I suck in a breath. "H—hi. How are you?"

He smiles at me, sunshine and crinkled eyes, but there's a shadow in those depths, one I don't remember from before. "I'm good. You?"

I bob my head. "Yep. Good." I can't believe it, that he's right here in front of me, touching me. I scramble for something more. I'm not ready for him to leave, not yet.

"Did you, um, were you able to, you know, after you left the room?"

I raise a shaky hand to my forehead and rub it, wincing.

Jesus. Way to go straight for the kill. Small talk would've been nice.

My question doesn't seem to bother him, though. It's almost like he expected it, which I guess makes sense. After all, that was our only interaction.

"Yeah. It worked every time after that."

Every time. The flare of jealousy is so overwhelming I almost fall down again. "That's great," I say through gritted teeth. "Your wife must be so happy."

His features darken. There's a slope to his shoulders now, like he carries a burden. "I'm divorced. As you might have guessed, there were other things wrong with my marriage, more than just that. In the end, nothing I did made it better. I tried, but it just…ended."

My heart aches for him. I know how much he believes in true love. "I'm so sorry," I tell him, meaning it with everything I have.

His throat works for a second. "How about you? How's everything going in that department?" T says it like we're speaking in code, which makes sense. This isn't exactly the kind of thing you talk about on a crowded subway train.

"Oh." Unconsciously, I run my finger over my latest tattoo. It's an arrow on my wrist, always pointing inward. Beneath it, two words: *be brave.* I trace the ink like a talisman before answering, "I don't know. I actually haven't had a chance to try."

He quirks his head at that, confusion flashing across his face. "You mean you haven't…since me?"

"No." One last grounding touch to the tattoo, then I pull myself up tall. "I realized I needed to work on loving myself first, before I could love someone else. So that's what I've been doing. Lots of therapy, self-reflection. It hasn't been easy, but I'm proud of myself. I think I've made a lot of progress."

This time, it's the smile I remember. The one that lights up his face. "I'm glad to hear that. Happy for you."

Finally, he releases me, takes a step back. My stomach drops with disappointment. This is it. Where we say good-bye for the last time.

But that's not what happens.

He sticks out his hand with a smile. "Hi, I'm Trevor."

T.

Trevor.

I shake his offered hand, loving how it engulfs my smaller one. "Kristi."

"Kristi." He rolls my name around in his mouth as if he likes the taste of it. "That's a good name." He moves closer, one step, and bends down to speak in my ear. His voice is warm, familiar.

"Well, Kristi, I'm new to this city, so you might have to pick the restaurant, but I was wondering if maybe I could take you to dinner?"

Something slides into place. A key fits into a lock.

I beam at him, and he grins back.

I tell Trevor, "I'd like that."

THE END

***

Thank You for Reading!

Dear Reader,

Can I ask for a HUGE favor? If you enjoyed this book, would you take a quick moment to leave a review?

I know your time is precious, but your words have an incredible impact. Reviews help other readers decide if this book is worth picking up—but they do more than that—they also tell retailers like Amazon to show it to more people, keeping stories like this alive and thriving. Every review, no matter how short, makes a real difference.

YOUR reviews help small indie authors like me compete with big publishers. If you love supporting authors who pour their hearts into their stories, this is one of the easiest and most meaningful ways to do it. Plus it's FREE! The only cost is a few minutes of your time— even a sentence or two on Amazon or Goodreads is a huge help.

Beyond that, I genuinely want to hear from you! What did you love? What made you stay up way too late flipping pages? Your feedback helps me craft even better books—the kind YOU want to read. I read every single review, and I appreciate you more than I can say.

Your review isn't just a favor—it's helping keep books like this alive.

From the bottom of my heart, THANK YOU.

XOXO, Lexi

Click link or scan QR code to review!

https://a.co/d/cdG4Tvd

***

Enjoyed Hold Me For Now? Craving more medical romance? I got you!

You need your next book boyfriend stat.

Paging Dr. Hart is *your next steamy, emotional obsession.*

She's an ice queen with walls built sky-high.

He's a charmer on a mission to melt her frozen heart.

When academic rivals are forced to live—and work—together, sparks fly, secrets unravel, and danger gets far too close to the heart.

If you love slow-burn tension, delicious enemies-to-lovers angst, and a dose of pulse-pounding medical suspense...**Paging Dr. Hart** will leave you breathless.

- **Grab it now and fall for your next favorite doctor.** https://a.co/d/4KDi2bz

This bestseller is available on Amazon and at most major booksellers. FREE to read on Kindle Unlimited.

- **Keep reading for a FREE sneak peek of Chapter One.**

Loving him might give her a heart attack.

Chapter 1

Present

Columbus, Ohio

Everyone's staring at me when I get the first mysterious text message. Because of course that's when it would happen. Not when I'm home alone or in my car or studying at the library.

Nope.

It has to be right then, when I'm about to start my presentation. The Mercy Hospital medical staff gathers in our auditorium every day at 8:00 a.m. for our morning educational conference. We take turns giving lectures about interesting cases, using them to teach the medical students and younger residents about disease processes and how to treat them.

Today it's my turn—my very first time. I'm not nervous, though. I mean, sure, my mouth is the Sahara Desert and my heart has crawled up into my throat, but I'm fine. *Totally fine.* At least that's what I tell myself as I gaze out into the sea of doctors. They look back with expressions that range from vague interest to frank boredom.

"Ladies and gentlemen," I begin. Heads swing my way, and conversation hushes. I've set my phone to silent. It sits on the podium, next to my laptop. I take a deep breath, about to continue my lecture, when the phone screen flashes and the phone vibrates so hard it skitters across the wooden surface. The noise startles me. I jolt and drop the microphone, which falls to the ground and lets out a squeal of feedback, like it's crying about its rough treatment.

Shit.

Heat warms my cheeks. I let out a shaky, apologetic smile. The audience stares back, waiting for me to get on with the show. While I'm on my hands and knees, fetching the microphone, I wonder who the message could be from. Hardly anyone ever calls or texts me. The phone is still vibrating rhythmically when I stand. Acutely aware of the crowd, I peer at the tiny screen. The text is from an unfamiliar number, but the image is all-too-familiar. It's a photo of the iconic Las Vegas sign. The one you see when you first drive into town, right before you reach the southern end of the neon-lit Strip.

"Welcome to fabulous Las Vegas, Nevada," it proclaims in bold, blood-red letters.

That's . . . odd.

I grew up in Las Vegas, but everyone I knew there is long gone. I scroll down. There's no message, no name. Nothing to explain who sent the picture or why. A chill shivers through me, the icy fingers of the past walking down my spine. I inhale a shaky breath and glance around, searching the shadows of the room, but find them empty. Nothing lurking. Still, foreboding settles low in my stomach, weighing me down.

With the audience watching, I can't react, so I carefully school my features. I need to nail this lecture. Hopefully, if I do well, it'll win me the Resident of the Month award. I've wanted that certificate, with its shiny gold seal, since I first started working here three years ago. It's physical proof that I've transformed. More importantly, I need it for the $1,000 bonus that comes along with it. I'll give this same presentation at a medical conference in a couple of months. It's an honor to speak there, one not usually given to residents. The money will let me stay at the swanky hotel at Disney World, where the conference is being held, instead of a cheap motel 30 miles down the road.

Another glance at the text stirs dark memories, which I bury. With a sigh, I set the phone aside, refusing to think of it again. It's time to focus. Luckily, or rather unluckily, I'm good at compartmentalizing.

I've had *lots* of practice.

"A 56-year-old male presents to the emergency department with blood in his urine," I begin. Methodically clicking through my slides one-by-one, I outline how the patient was diagnosed with renal cancer. A CAT scan appears on the screen. With my pointer, I demonstrate how cancerous tendrils extend from the kidney and worm their way up into the biggest vein in the body, the inferior vena cava.

"For renal cancer," I explain, "we use tumor staging to help define the extent of disease and prognosis. Because the tumor extends outside the kidney, this patient is stage T3c." A click later shows photos from the surgery when the kidney was removed. Nearing the end of my talk, I discuss the patient's treatment and what imaging we will use for follow-up. This man will get repeat CAT scans every six months to make sure he remains cancer-free.

I pause to catch my breath, since I've been talking nonstop, and survey the audience. Everyone's still alert, and most are paying attention, which is all I can ask for. These early-morning presentations are often dry. Even I've had to fight to stay awake in this dark room when it was someone else up here lecturing.

"I'd like to open the floor to questions now," I say. There are a few raised hands from the crowd, asking about the man's long-term chance of reoccurrence and treatment options, which I answer easily. Relief floods through me. The finish line is in sight. There've been no technical difficulties. I haven't stuttered or said anything embarrassing. I give myself a mental pat on the back and prepare to end the presentation.

That's when a hand shoots up into the air.

It's a man, about my age, with ruffled brown hair, dark straight brows, and a square jaw. He sits next to Dr. Washburn, my residency director and boss. There's something mesmerizing about him. Something difficult to define but makes it hard to look away. It's partly his eyes, which are stunning, an unusually light color, warm amber like a glass of whiskey when the sunlight filters through it.

I've never seen him before.

I'd remember a face like that.

I nod politely. "You have a question?"

The man's voice is deep, carrying easily through the auditorium. "Yes. It's about the tumor staging. You said it was stage T3c?"

"That's correct." I frown, wondering where he's going with this.

"I think it's actually T3b. T3c is when the cancer is in the inferior vena cava but goes *above* the diaphragm. T3b is when it stays *below* the diaphragm. In those images you showed, the tumor was below."

Flustered, my normally orderly mind reels.

"Um—give me a minute." Time stretches out as I frantically search through the notebook where I wrote my research to prepare for this lecture.

Someone in the crowd coughs. Chairs squeak as people shift. The projector overhead whirs, its fan turning on. My breath comes in brief spurts. Hands shaking, I flip through the pages.

Where is it? Where is it?

Ah. It's there in my handwriting.

T3b.

The handsome stranger is right.

Crap. There goes my award.

Heat rushes up my neck to splash across my cheeks. Humiliation gives way to fury. I'm mad at myself for making the error, but I'm also angry at *him*. Why would he correct me in front of everyone? Who even does that? I should have known. No man can be that pretty without also being cruel. Every eye is trained on me, waiting to see how I'll respond.

I swallow around the boulder in my throat. "It is T3b. I must have typed it wrong. I apologize."

"No problem," he says graciously.

Now, I hate him. First for pointing out my mistake and second for acting like it's not a big deal.

To me, it's a *very* big deal indeed . . .

Available on Amazon and at most major book sellers. FREE to read on Kindle Unlimited!

Get it now! https://a.co/d/4KDi2bz

***

Also by Melissa Dymond/Lexi Davis

- *Holiday Star-* a celebrity holiday romance https://a.co/d/53YUnxd

- *Holiday Wedding-* a holiday romance with suspense https://a.co/d/39b6gyh

- *Paging Dr. Hart-* a medical romance with suspense https://a.co/d/bvCcctp

- *Deeply Examined-* a spicy dark medical romance https://a.co/d/

6CDvmQh

Chapter Fourteen

Acknowledgments

Acknowledgments

Hello, Dear Reader,

The most important person I want to thank is YOU. There would be no book without you. Please know how much I appreciate you taking a chance on an indie author like me. Thanks also to those of you who leave a review, post on social media, reach out with an email or a DM, and recommend my books to your friends and family. Those extra steps make all the difference.

If I can be known for one thing as an author, it's that I write for you, my readers. It's your happiness I'm after. The ability to entertain you. Make you laugh, cry, or swoon. That's what I want, and I'll do anything to make sure you're smiling by the time you read the words "The End."

I'm fortunate that I have a talented team who help make this book a hundred times better. Thank you to my editor Lura Dymond. I couldn't do this without you.

Thank you to my personal assistant, Hayley Faryna, who has completely transformed my Instagram page into something gorgeous. Beyond that, she beta reads, strategizes, and occasionally talks me off a ledge. Thanks to Maude Levesque, who also helps with social media and is just about the nicest person ever. Mikala Beers is another social media genius and Sara Usera is a huge help with advertising.

Thanks to my beta readers: Diza Parker, Jane Litherland, Celina Lyles. Your insight helped make this book better.

Thanks to book communities on social media, especially Bookstagram, BookTok, and BookTube. I love connecting with readers there! @authorlexidavis